# FOR BARNEY,

### who could balance five blocks on his chin while lying on his back and slowly wagging his tail.

Books published by Running Press are available at special discounts for bulk purchases in the United States by corporations, institutions, and other organizations. For more information, please contact the Special Markets Department at the Perseus Books Group, 2300 Chestnut Street, Suite 200, Philadelphia, PA 19103, or call (800) 810-4145, ext. 5000, or e-mail special.markets@perseusbooks.com.

ISBN 978-0-7624-4429-8
Library of Congress Control Number: 2011937692

E-book ISBN 978-0-7624-4533-2

9  8  7  6  5  4  3  2
Digit on the right indicates the number of this printing

Designed by Frances J. Soo Ping Chow
Edited by Marlo Scrimizzi
Typography: Love Ya Like A Sister and Neutra

Published by Running Press Kids
An Imprint of Running Press Book Publishers
A Member of the Perseus Books Group
2300 Chestnut Street
Philadelphia, PA 19103-4371

Visit us on the web!
www.runningpress.com

# PERCY and Tum Tum
## A Tale of Two Dogs
### BY JEN HILL

RP|KIDS
PHILADELPHIA · LONDON

**In the little old town** of Riveredge Waterwood, there was an animal shelter. And in that shelter lived a cushy, cuddly, roly-poly dog named TumTum.

So cushy and cuddly was he that people could not resist going inside to play with him. TumTum had many talents and dazzled everyone he met with his charming personality.

It wasn't long before a family came to take TumTum home with them.
It was both a happy and sad occasion for all.

"Goodbye, TumTum," they said. "Promise us you'll come back and visit soon!"

TumTum's new family was eager to welcome him to his new home.

But there was one member of the family who would not be charmed by
this newcomer. . . .

His name was Percy.

TumTum loved to make new friends. When he introduced himself to Percy, TumTum greeted him with a little dance.

Everyone thought it was an adorable gesture, but Percy just sneered. He would never stoop to be friends with such a silly dog.

For Percy was serious and dignified by nature. To him, the clownish TumTum was nothing but a dopey nuisance.

It galled Percy to see TumTum receiving so much attention.

*They only liked him because of his big fluffy coat, he thought.*

TumTum knew many amusing tricks. His amazing performances drew in large crowds, and he was often the life of the party.

Percy didn't think much of TumTum's talents. "I can do that," he scoffed.

Percy played pranks on TumTum that weren't very funny.

Sometimes he was downright mean.

But TumTum never let it bother him.

As TumTum accepted the "Pet of the Year" award at the summer block party, Percy looked on in disgust. Enough was ENOUGH!

Then Percy had a brilliant idea which made him snicker so hard he almost fell over. He ran home as fast as his stubby little legs could carry him.

That night, as everyone in the house lay sound asleep,
Percy crept downstairs until he reached the snoring TumTum.

TumTum was dreaming of chasing butterflies through a meadow and did not hear the *snip snip* of the scissors on his big fluffy coat.

Percy was very satisfied with himself when he finished the haircut. He slinked back upstairs and soon fell asleep, and dreamed he was king of all the neighborhood dogs.

But the next morning, things did not go according to plan. . . .

TumTum awoke and went out for his morning walk.
*Something was different*, he thought.

Those who saw him did a double take, for without
his big fluffy coat, TumTum was hard to recognize.
But his goofy smile gave him away.

The neighborhood girls thought he looked adorable.

The old lady next door knitted him a sweater for chilly days.
The young men nodded with approval.

The Rottweilers and the pit bulls admired TumTum's daring new look, as did the poodles and the Chihuahuas. Even the cats liked it.

The townspeople were inspired by TumTum's new look, and they lined up to get their hair cut just like his.

*It wasn't his fur after all,* thought Percy. It was TumTum's sparkling personality everyone adored.

TumTum, who was new in town, had made many friends. And Percy, he suddenly realized, didn't have any. *Maybe it was time to give TumTum a chance*, he thought. And he knew just how to begin his apology. . . .

Percy had a new plan. He settled himself in front of the mirror and gave himself a haircut, just like the one he'd given to TumTum.

Percy had gained two things that day: a new look . . .

. . . and a new friend.